Baby Mickey's Book of Opposites

A GOLDEN BOOK · NEW YORK
Western Publishing Company, Inc.
Racine, Wisconsin 53404

It is *dark* outside.
Baby Mickey is asleep in his cozy crib.

Now morning has come. It is *light* outside and time for Baby Mickey to get up. Today he is going to the beach!

Baby Mickey sees his friends at the beach. They are having fun playing in the sand and in the water.

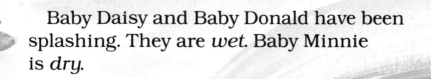

Baby Daisy and Baby Donald have been splashing. They are *wet*. Baby Minnie is *dry*.

Baby Mickey and Baby Minnie build
a sandcastle.
Baby Minnie makes a *tall* tower.
Baby Mickey makes a *short* tower.

Baby Donald and Baby Daisy
each have a pail.
Baby Donald's pail is *new*.
Baby Daisy's pail is *old*.
Both pails hold lots of water.

Now Baby Donald's pail is *empty*.
Baby Daisy's pail is still *full*.

Time for lunch!
Baby Mickey has a *big* apple.
Baby Minnie has a *little* apple.

Baby Mickey has lost his seashell.
He is very *sad*.

Baby Minnie finds the seashell.
Now Baby Mickey is *happy* again.

Baby Goofy and Baby Pluto are playing *inside* a beach tent.
Baby Mickey is *outside* the tent.

Baby Donald and Baby Daisy are
watching the boats race far out in the
water.
The red boat is *first*.
The green boat is *last*.

Now it is time to pack up and go home.
Baby Mickey and Baby Minnie have
special beach bags for their toys.
Baby Mickey's bag is *open*.
Baby Minnie's bag is *closed*.

The light at the corner is red.
Baby Mickey knows that this means *stop*.
They must wait until it changes.

Now the light is green.
Baby Mickey knows that this
means *go* and they may cross
the street.

Baby Mickey had a good time at the
beach. And he has brought home his pretty
seashell. When he puts it to his ear, he can
hear the sound of the ocean. It reminds him
of his nice day.